Hoof on the Roof

'Hoof on the Roof'
An original concept by Cath Jones
© Cath Jones

Illustrated by Gisela Bohorquez

Published by MAVERICK ARTS PUBLISHING LTD
Studio 11, City Business Centre, 6 Brighton Road,
Horsham, West Sussex, RH13 5BB
© Maverick Arts Publishing Limited August 2020
+44 (0)1403 256941

A CIP catalogue record for this book is available at the British Library.

ISBN 978-1-84886-684-3

www.maverickbooks.co.uk

Green

This book is rated as: Green Band (Guided Reading)
This story is mostly decodable at Letters and Sounds Phase 5.
Up to five non-decodable story words are included.

Hoof on the Roof

by Cath Jones

illustrated by
Gisela Bohorquez

Lizzy loved eating grass. She liked grass that was long, green and fresh. But the grass in her field was short.

"I want to explore," said Lizzy.

The other cows helped Lizzy leave.

"Be careful," called the cows,

as Lizzy trotted off down the road.

Soon Lizzy came to a farmhouse.

The roof was made of grass!

She mooed happily.

Lizzy spotted a ladder.

But Lizzy was big and heavy.

SNAP!

The ladder broke in half!

"Sorry!" said Lizzy.

She looked up at the
yummy grass roof.

Lizzy knocked on the farm door.

Hooves were good for knocking!

But nobody came out.

Lizzy sniffed.

The grass smelled so good!

She decided to borrow the digger.

But Lizzy's hooves made it tricky
to brake.

Lizzy needed help to get onto the roof.

She set off to tell the other cows.

The cows were happy to see Lizzy.

"The farmer has a yummy grass roof,"
she said. "Come and see it!"

The cows worked together
to get onto the roof.

1, 2, 3, UP!

Lizzy and the cows ate the grass.

They danced with joy.

Clomp, clomp, clomp!

The farmer came out to see
what the noise was.

When the farmer saw the cows,

he was amazed.

"Thank you for eating my grass," said the farmer. "You are better than a lawnmower!"

The farmer built a ramp for the cows so they could always get to the grass.

Lizzy and the cows were happy on the roof. The farmer was happy too. He did not have to cut his grass!

Quiz

1. The grass in Lizzy's field was...
a) Long
b) Dirty
c) Short

2. Why did Lizzy break the ladder?
a) She was big and heavy
b) She jumped on it
c) She tripped on it

3. The grass on the roof smelled so...
a) Bad
b) Smelly
c) Good

4. How did the cows get onto the roof?
a) With a digger
b) With a ladder
c) By working together

5. What did the farmer build for the cows?
a) A slide
b) A ramp
c) A barn

Turn over for answers

Book Bands for Guided Reading

The Institute of Education book banding system is a scale of colours that reflects the various levels of reading difficulty. The bands are assigned by taking into account the content, the language style, the layout and phonics. Word, phrase and sentence level work is also taken into consideration.

Maverick Early Readers are a bright, attractive range of books covering the pink to white bands. All of these books have been book banded for guided reading to the industry standard and edited by a leading educational consultant.

To view the whole Maverick Readers scheme, visit our website at

www.maverickearlyreaders.com

Or scan the QR code above to view our scheme instantly!

Quiz Answers: 1c, 2a, 3c, 4c, 5b